1 9 SEP 2022

2 2 MAR 2024

3 0 APR 2024

Please return/renew this item by the last date shown.
Items may also be renewed by the internet*

https://library.eastriding.gov.uk

* Please note a PIN will be required to access this service
- this can be obtained from your library

For Jack, William and Alistair with love

Marion Gamble

The Westwood Troll

AUSTIN MACAULEY
PUBLISHERS LTD.

A CIP catalogue record for this title is available from the British Library.

ISBN 9781785545191 (Paperback)
ISBN 9781785545207 (Hardback)

www.austinmacauley.com

First Published (2015)
Austin Macauley Publishers Ltd.
25 Canada Square
Canary Wharf
London
E14 5LQ

Printed and bound in Great Britain

The Westwood Troll lives under the hill inside a small cave by the Black Mill.

He lurks in the bushes by the gate,
that is where he lies in wait.

When cars drive over the cattle grid
the Troll gives a low "G R O W L"
which frightens the children and makes them howl!

They hear his growl as they go past.
"How does he look?" the children ask.

"What do you think?
Try and guess."

"He's short and fat with a baldy head
I wonder if his name is Fred?"

"He has big feet and a hairy nose,
he looks quite scruffy with raggedy clothes."

"He has staring eyes and big ugly teeth,
I wonder if his name is Keith?"

"The Westwood Troll is a curious fellow
I think he wears a coat of yellow."

"Will he catch us, does he bite,
does he lurk there in the dark at night?"

"Will he catch us as we drive by?"
"We had better go fast he just might try."

You had better watch out if you go flying a kite
or ride across the Westwood on your bike.

If you go for a picnic on the Westwood beware of the Troll, you really should.

"What does the Troll eat?" the children ask.

"What do you think?
Try and guess."

Wild berries and fruit or some kind of meat,
a rabbit or squirrel to make a pie?
He can't catch us, even though he might try!

If you go walking across the Westwood today,
look out for the Troll as you go on your way.

He roams over the fairway and around Burton Bushes,
as you stroll by there he could be hiding in the rushes.

Some days when he is happy he sings a song,
it's fun to sing and it's not very long.

"Fold de roll, I'm a troll,
fold de roll, I'm a jolly old troll.
Fold de roll, I'm a troll,
today I'm feeling very droll."

When out on the Westwood, children beware.
look out for the Troll hiding in his lair.

His eyes may be dim and he's not very bright,
but be especially careful crossing the Westwood at night.

If you should see the Troll you had better start running,
he might try and catch you, he's very cunning.

No one ever sees the Westwood Troll
and nobody really knows his name.

They have heard his growl and heard his song.
They do not stay near the cattle grid long.

They don't go near his cave under the hill
but as far as we know he lives there still.

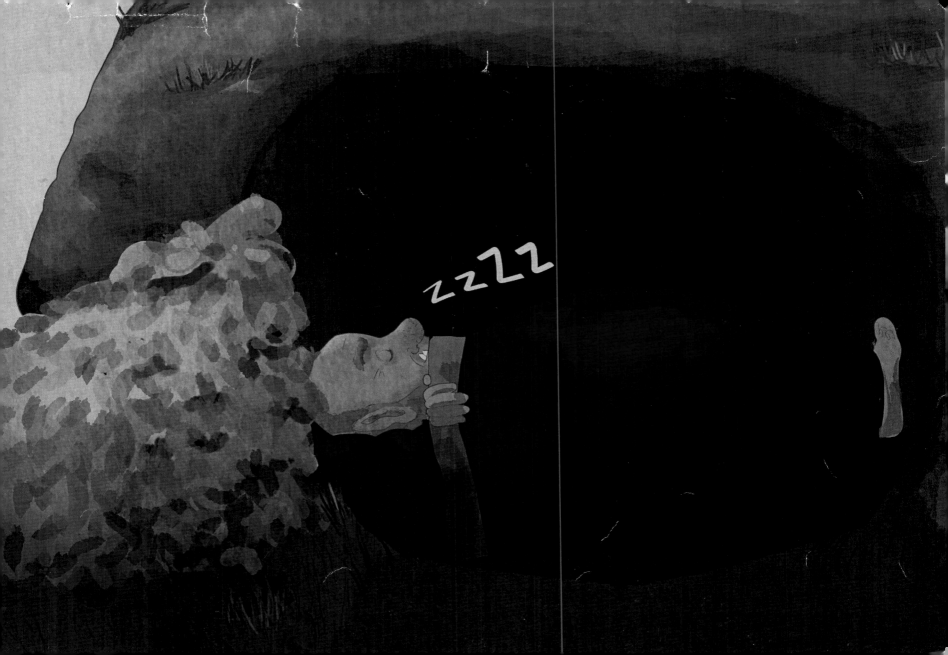